DATE DUE

GAYLORD			PRINTED IN U.S.A.

Don't Call Me Toad!

Don't Call Me Toad!

Mary Francis Shura

Illustrated by Jacqueline Rogers

G.P. PUTNAM'S SONS
NEW YORK

Library of Congress Cataloging-in-Publication Data
Shura, Mary Francis, 1923– Don't call me Toad! /
Mary Francis Shura : illustrated by Jacqueline Rogers. p. cm.
Summary: An uneasy friendship with the strange,
constantly angry new girl in her neighborhood leads
eleven-year-old Jamie Potter to discover a hidden cache of
money and stolen jewelry. [1. Friendship – Fiction.
2. Buried treasure – Fiction. 3. Mystery and detective stories.]
I. Rogers, Jackie, ill. II. Title. [PZ7.S55983Do 1988]
[Fic] – dc19   88-26336 CIP AC
ISBN 0-399-21706-1

10 9 8 7 6 5 4

For

Nancy and Martha

with love

Contents

Don't Call Me Toad!

1

Haverhill House

A toad, according to the little dictionary Mom gave me to improve my spelling, is a froglike land animal. I think of toads as having warts, catching flies, and squatting in dark hidden places to stare out at you with big moist eyes. I can't imagine any eleven-year-old girl wanting to have anything to do with a person who would hang a nickname like that on her, especially when that person was cross and rude besides.

That's why, when I met Dinah Dobbins on that wet November Tuesday, I not only didn't ever want to see her again, I didn't care what happened to her or her little runaway brother. I certainly had no intention of letting her get me involved in a mystery that would scare me half to death and change the whole way I felt about hurting.

You see, I really hate to be hurt, and I had figured out my own way to avoid it long before I met Dinah Dobbins. I learned my lessons with Mindy Carlson and Peter Miller.

Mindy Carlson was the first friend who really hurt me, even if it wasn't her own fault. Mindy and I went to kindergarten and first grade together and played all the time. We started on bikes with training wheels together and took them off the same week. She was wonderful to play with. Every time we ran out of things to do, Mindy would come up with some new game. Her ideas were wonderful, like making doll faces out of the wrinkled apples we found in the orchard grass. But her dad was Air Force and he got transferred, and Mindy moved away.

Then there was Peter Miller. He didn't care that I was a girl, we were friends just the same. He lived down the street from me and we explored the game preserve and searched along the banks of the Missouri River for the hidden tunnels that smugglers and river pirates were supposed to have dug under a towering old mansion called Haverhill House. But

Peter's dad was Air Force too, and just when I was sure we were going to find the tunnel entrance Peter's dad was transferred, and they moved away.

Because Riverton is the closest town to a big Air Force base, we get those kids all the time. When Peter left with his family, I promised myself that never again was I going to make friends with any Air Force kid who would come and be important to me and then leave me lonesome and hurting once more. And I never have. All through fifth grade and the first two months of this year I haven't even had any special friends at school. I've spent most of my time at home with my dog and my rabbits or helping my folks at our grocery store.

Then Dinah Dobbins jumped out of the bushes at Haverhill House and called me a toad, and I quit getting my way about anything.

The rain had begun about noon that day. Naturally I got caught at school without a raincoat—and without my bicycle. None of us kids have bicycles any more, because one night in September thieves came into Riverton and stole every decent bike in the entire town, including mine, which was brand new because I got it on my eleventh birthday in August.

Winter comes early in Nebraska and by three-thirty, when school was out, it was almost dark. The rain had turned to sleet. That wouldn't have been so awful except that on Tuesdays and Thursdays I don't get to go straight home from school. Instead, I have to stop by my dad's grocery store to pick up an order for Miss Foster.

Our grocery store doesn't usually deliver but Dad makes an exception for Miss Foster, who is old and lives in Haverhill House up above our street. She's lived there ever since Dad can remember and used to be sprightly enough to raise her own flowers and walk down to the store for what she needed. Then she had a fall and had to use a cane to walk, so Dad started having me take her groceries to her. I have kept doing it, even though she's not alone any more. For this past year a young writer and historian named Mr. Jeremy has been boarding with her.

Haverhill House is big and white and rears up like a castle from the top of the hill. It is trimmed with all sorts of fancy woodwork and has a little balcony around the top that people called a "widow's walk." It's set on about five acres of apple and pear orchard. An old man named Bird used to keep the grounds for Miss Foster, but after he died Miss Foster just had people come in by the day when she needed work done. Since none of them knew how to prune fruit trees, the orchard was already a mess before Mr. Jeremy came to live in her house.

Mr. Jeremy hired a man named Tony Buck for Miss Foster. Mr. Buck moved into the tack room in the stable where Mr. Bird had lived. Mr. Buck keeps the lawn mowed and the snow shoveled off in winter, but he doesn't work nearly as hard as Mr. Bird did. The orchard is still all weeds and tangle, with deep grass and fallen fruit.

I agree with my mom and dad that it's too bad to see that lovely old orchard go to brambles, but it is sure nice for the animals that find refuge there. Besides rabbits, raccoons, and opossums, there are a lot more skunks than any neighborhood needs. The bramble protects them and they only have to climb down the cliff beyond the stables to be at the river, where they can get water. I love to go back into the orchard. Except when somebody has scared up one of those skunks, it always smells good and fruity there.

Mr. Jeremy is writing a history book about Riverton during the opening of the West. Dad has always told me how proud I should be of my town's history. We talked about Riverton a lot when Mr. Jeremy first came. Riverton is right on the Missouri River, which is famous for being hard to navigate.

Yet whole families came up here on boats and rafts before steam engines were even invented. The town did a thriving business in equipping pioneers who were going on to Oregon or California. You can still see WELLS FARGO written in faded paint on one of the warehouses down by the wharf. Like my dad, the members of all the old families in town have been thrilled to help provide historical material. Mr. Jeremy spends most of his time interviewing the old-timers in town, when he's not researching at the library.

I'm proud enough about the town history, but personally I think he'd get a better book if he wrote about the river pirates who built Haverhill House a hundred years ago. They dug tunnels that led back to the river and hid their loot in them until boats came to take the stuff away. People only gossiped about those tunnels until the Prohibition days when it was against the law to have any kind of liquor in America. Then federal agents caught smugglers using those old hiding places to store illegal whiskey and sealed off the entrances so nobody could find them and get in.

I was wet and cold that day. All the way up the long brick walk that leads to Haverhill House I kept thinking about making myself hot cocoa when I got home. I decided I would change my clothes from the skin out and maybe even take a hot shower.

A wide porch runs all along the front and west side of Miss Foster's house. That day it was littered with wet leaves from the huge black walnut tree that leans against the roof. As I raised the knocker to let Miss Foster know I was there, I heard something rattle on the floor of the porch behind me. You can bet I jumped and looked around to see what was after me. Right away, I decided it was only walnuts being blown off the tree and rolling across the wooden boards, but I still had a shivery feeling until Miss Foster switched on the porch light and I heard her turning the key to open the door.

After I set the groceries down in her kitchen, Miss Foster invited me to stay a while and dry off but I told her I'd better get home. When she closed the door behind me, she left the porch light on. I looked over at the darkness under the tree where I had heard the funny noise, but my eyes were blinded from the light. I could only see the shadow of the tree limbs swaying and hear the shutters on the second floor banging in the wind. If the path hadn't been so slick and wet, I would have run home. Instead I hunched over and walked really fast.

Just as I reached the end of the walk, a figure in

a shapeless poncho stepped out from behind the lilac bushes. This person was wearing a wide-brimmed hat that streamed water onto its poncho, and it just stood there, blocking my path. It scared me, jumping out like that. It always makes me mad to be scared.

The minute the figure spoke I knew this was another girl. She stared up at Haverhill House where the light was still shining on the porch. She had to be Air Force because I hadn't seen her before, and I know all the kids in town that are my age. "What is that place?" she asked.

"A house," I said. "Haverhill House."

Even though the light wasn't very good, her eyes gave me a funny, shivery feeling. "Is that the pirate's house?" she asked.

"It used to be in the old days," I told her. "Miss Foster lives there now."

"I don't like it," she snapped. "Did you see a boy up there?"

"What kind of a boy?" I asked. It was a stupid question, but I was really startled at the cross way she spoke and the tense, tight way she held herself, as if she were just looking for somebody to pick a fight with.

"Don't be such a toad," she barked. "A human

boy, what did you think? He's my—brother. He's little and tubby and fast as lightning and he got away from me."

Toad! What kind of a thing is that to call anyone?

Before I could catch my breath, she barked at me again. "So you saw him or you didn't, speak up!"

"I didn't," I said, glaring at her. I might have told her about the funny noise I thought I'd heard on the porch if she hadn't been so rude. Mindy never was rude and neither was Peter, but a lot of Air Force kids acted like this one and I was pretty sick of it. Just because they've lived all over the world doesn't give them any right to call Riverton a hick town and sneer at us kids who live here all the time.

The girl looked up the path toward Haverhill House again and then along our street, which has only ordinary houses like the one I live in. "Okay," she said, as if she were offering me some kind of a challenge. "Where would you go, if you were a boy?"

"I'd go somewhere inside where it's warm. But then again, I'm not a little kid and crazy enough to run away in this kind of weather."

She looked at me again. "However old you are, *you're* out in it." Then, without another word, she turned and stamped off down the street, that big poncho billowing out behind her.

I stood a minute staring after her. Why would anybody be that angry just because a kid had strayed away? Why wasn't she calling the boy's name instead of jumping out of bushes and insulting absolute strangers like me?

I glanced back up at Haverhill House. If the movement I thought I had seen on the end of the porch was a little kid, he could get himself into real trouble. Right on the other side of the porch are some terrible brambles where the raspberries grow in summer. The buildings just beyond have rotten floors, and the door to the root cellar is broken down so a child could fall in there. The stable with the tack room where Mr. Buck lives is the only structure back there in decent shape.

I decided it wouldn't hurt me to go up and check around the porch for the kid. I wasn't *that* cold and wet, and Mom and Dad wouldn't be home until after they closed the store at six. Until I was ten, they had a baby sitter come to stay with me after school. It was awful. The sitters were either high-school girls who only wanted to watch TV and eat or they were older ladies who wanted to talk to me about their very bad health or their grandchildren, who didn't have any of my bad habits. Finally my folks and I made a deal. If I did my homework and helped start dinner, I would be allowed to stay by myself and be treated like a grownup.

Miss Foster had left the light on for me to walk down the path. It flicked off when I was halfway back up the hill. I saw a dim yellowish glow from the inside parlor. Other than that, the only light was high up on the east side of the house in the room where Mr. Jeremy does his writing when he isn't out visiting around town in his van with the charcoal-glass windows.

Instead of going up on the porch, I walked around it under the walnut tree. The ground was uneven and knobby under my feet. I squinted to see better in the dark as I began to circle the house. I decided to check the root cellar first, because that's the most dangerous place.

I had passed the raspberry bramble and the smokehouse when I felt the prickle that comes on the back of my neck when there's somebody else around and I don't know who it is. Before I could turn, I was grabbed from behind and jerked clear off my feet.

"Now"—the voice was gruff but familiar—"let's get a look at you."

"Mr. Buck," I wailed. "It's me, Janie Potter." My own voice squeaked so it didn't even sound like me.

"Sure it is!" he said, his voice still angry. Then he pulled me over and flipped on the light outside the smokehouse to peer at me. "Well, I'll be dogged. It is you, Janie. And it *is* the day for Tuesday groceries." Then he shook his head a little. "Too bad. I figured I had caught the prowler who's been nosing around here in the dark." He stopped and looked at me. "Maybe that was you before and I just thought it was some stranger? Are you looking for something around here in back?"

"Someone," I told him, pulling my jacket down. "I'm looking for a little boy who ran off."

"Whose little boy?"

"Some Air Force kid. I just met his sister and I thought he might have come up here."

"Well, he hasn't any business up here if he did. It's no place for a little kid to go wandering around at night." He peered at me again in the light. "Want to look around some more?"

"Let her find her own brother," I told him. "It isn't any of my business, anyway." I had started shaking all over the minute he grabbed me. I just wanted to be home and warm.

Since I'm an only child, I've never had a sister.

But if I had a sister who was as rude and angry as the girl in the poncho, I'd probably run away too, and I sure wouldn't want some busybody helping her find me.

2
Rabbit Food

My dog, Missy, was whining a welcome while I fished out my key to unlock the door. I'd lost about three keys to our house before Mom started making me wear one around my neck on a chain. We never used to have to lock our doors at all in Riverton. Then we started having a crime wave. Robbers began coming to town and breaking into houses and stealing things out of garages and barns. Mostly they took stereo equipment or silverware or expensive tools, but the worst was that time they carted off every bike in town—including my beautiful silver one with the dark-red racing stripes.

As soon as I got indoors, I gave Missy a good loving and made cocoa.

We didn't choose Missy, she chose us. She came to our back door during a January blizzard and wouldn't go away. When Dad decided he should take her to the shelter, I cried and Mom wouldn't talk to him, so we had a dog. It's fun to have a dog with lots of different ancestors. Missy is black like a Labrador Retriever and likes to swim in the river, even when there is ice. She walks in a lope like a German Shepherd and really is a good watchdog. Hidden in there somewhere is some mysterious little kind of dog because she really likes to sit on couches with you, and would get on your lap if it were big enough.

Missy isn't allowed on the couch but I was cold enough to make this an emergency. I let her get up beside me under a blanket while I drank a whole pot of cocoa and tried to warm up. We stayed there maybe an hour.

I was thinking seriously about getting out from under the blanket long enough to reach for my schoolbooks when Missy let out a big throaty growl. She shook off the blanket and jumped from the couch. Her toenails skittered as she tried to work up speed on the bare floor. When she finally got some traction, she charged the back door, throwing her body against it and barking loudly enough to deafen a person. I opened the door and she plunged into the back yard.

I called for her to come back. When she didn't, I picked up the warm blanket to wrap around myself while I looked out the window in the kitchen door. It was too dark to see anything except the shining reflection of the house lights on the puddles. When I flipped on the outside light, I realized that river fog had filled up our back yard while Missy and I were snuggled on the couch. The floodlight didn't cut the fog at all and I couldn't see anything.

We get a lot of fog when the seasons change. It comes up from the river like wet smoke and fingers in around the buildings close to the ground. Noises sound different in fog, and lights from houses down the street become blurs of yellow.

The minute Missy went out the door, she'd plunged off around the house, barking like fury. That same minute she disappeared, and I could only hear the barking, hollow the way it comes in fog.

That made three separate times I had been spooked in a single afternoon, and it made me mad. It also scared me for my rabbits, and that made me even madder. A lot of the land along the river is a bird sanctuary and wildlife preserve, and the coyotes and foxes sometimes come prowling into town. Every animal that eats other animals likes rabbits. I grabbed my slicker and hat and went out to check on my pets.

I yelled for Missy to come back about six times before she figured out I was serious about it. Even when she finally obeyed, she appeared out of the mist with her tail down and a growl still rumbling in her throat.

Whatever had spooked her was gone. The rabbits were fine, all balled against the back of their cages to get out of the wet wind. I took Missy inside and told her to shut up or I would lock her in the basement. It was a quarter to six. I hadn't started my homework or even checked the bulletin board to see what Mom wanted me to do about supper.

And it was all the fault of that rude Air Force kid in the poncho.

At dinner I told Mom and Dad about running into a girl looking for a lost little boy at the foot of Miss Foster's walk.

"I hope she found the child," Mom said.

I shrugged. "I don't know, but I didn't see her again."

"That must be the family Bennett rented his house to," Dad told Mom. "He told me he was renting his place to a sergeant. The moving van was unloading when I left for the store this morning."

Mom nodded. "I understand they have two children, a girl and a boy. The mother was a teacher over in Germany. It certainly would be nice if the girl is the right age to play with you, Jane."

Dad laughed. "The grocery store grapevine coils again." Mom just grinned at him. They laugh about the way you hear more news running a grocery store than you would if you were editor of the paper.

"If that's the girl, I don't intend to have anything to do with her," I told Mom. "She's mad."

"Jane," Mom said, looking shocked. "That's an awful thing to say about somebody you barely met."

"I don't mean mad like crazy," I explained. "But she was really bad mannered and rude, and she acted angry when I hadn't done anything to her. I wouldn't have wanted her to find me, if I were that little kid."

"Maybe she was scared she wasn't going to find him," Dad put in, winking at me. "I know somebody else who gets angry when she's scared."

I ducked my head to hide a smile. Dad was right. "But I don't get rude and insult strangers," I told him.

I didn't mention her calling me a toad. It was embarrassing enough to remember her saying it.

I am supposed to do three jobs every morning before I leave for school. I load breakfast dishes into the dishwasher, let Missy run in the yard, and feed my rabbits.

We had poached eggs on toast that next morning. I love poached eggs but I hate to clean up after them. If you don't get all the egg off the plate before you put it in the dishwasher, it cooks to yellow leather.

"Run fast, Missy," I shouted, letting her out the back door for her exercise while I went to feed the rabbits.

The yard was sodden from the rain. It made sucking sounds whenever I took a step. Dark wet leaves torn from the trees by the wind were pasted against the side of the garage and littered the whole yard. I groaned. Guess who was going to get to rake those up?

My rabbit hutch is built against the side of a little building that used to be a smokehouse when Grandma and Grandpa lived here. Since we don't kill pigs and make hams out of them, we use it as storage for tools and the lawn mower and stuff like that.

Buckwheat was an Easter present about five years ago. When he got big, I talked Dad into the second rabbit, a girl named Downie. By the next Easter, we had to build hutches all up the side of the smokehouse and add an overhang to the roof to keep out the rain and snow. Rabbits make neat pets. They know you and like you. They come and push their noses against the wire to touch your hands.

I had filled their water troughs and was putting the last of the food in when I noticed something sticking through the wire of Buckwheat's cage. It was green, but brighter than a leaf. I tugged it out and looked at it without really believing my eyes. As ridiculous as it sounds, I was holding a twenty dollar bill. Andrew Jackson's head had been partly nibbled away.

Who in the world would feed a twenty dollar bill to a rabbit? And Buckwheat hadn't even liked it much, because he left more than he ate.

3

Orange Sneakers

By the time I got to the door of my sixth-grade homeroom that morning, I could hear that Miss Harvey was already talking. I hadn't heard the tardy bell, but it's hard to listen and run really fast at the same time. I hate tardy marks on my grade card but, even more than that, I hate the way everybody stares when you walk in late. I tiptoed up the aisle as quietly as I could. I didn't look at anyone, hoping I might be temporarily invisible.

I wasn't.

Miss Harvey raised her eyebrows at me and went on talking. "As I was saying before Jane Potter gave us her imitation of a tardy student unsuccessfully trying to sneak in after the late bell, we have a new member in our class. I'd like you to meet . . ."

The new student was a show-off. Miss Harvey barely had the name "Dinah Dobbins" out of her mouth before the girl was on her feet, standing up very straight beside her desk as if she owned not only that piece of floor but the whole room, and maybe the world.

Although she wasn't anything like pretty, she had somehow started with nothing and made it into something. By nothing I mean she was all the same color—short straight brown hair, brown eyes, and a sort of tanned look to her skin. Her clothes made her look different. Most of us girls wear jeans, some in light colors and some regular blue. We wear blouses or shirts with something advertised on them, like Disneyland or a camp we've gone to, or a rock star we like. Not this girl. She had on putty-colored floppy pants with all sorts of pockets down the sides of the legs, as if she were a mechanic or a paratrooper. She had pulled a bulky orange sweat shirt down over those crazy pants. That orange was bright enough to make my eyes water, and her sneakers were the same horrible color. I looked the other way. I had never seen orange sneakers before, and I was absolutely certain I didn't want to again.

"Yes, Ma'am?" she asked.

The minute she spoke I recognized her voice. This was the girl who had come out of the bushes at Haverhill House.

Miss Harvey hesitated. In our school, kids usually sit in their seats to answer instead of standing at attention in the aisle like that. Miss Harvey seemed at a loss for a moment. Then she 'asked, "Would you like to tell the class where you're from, Dinah?"

Dinah Dobbins smiled in a funny way with the sides of her mouth pulled down. "I'm from just about everywhere," she said. "I'm an Air Force brat."

The class stirred. When the kids squirm in those old chairs, it starts a chorus of metallic shrieks that drives Miss Harvey crazy. She has been known to yell. (Scraping a fingernail on the blackboard gets the same reaction from Mr. Adams in Language Arts.) Miss Harvey frowned and took a firm grip on her self-control. "Sit still, class," she said. "And Dinah, that is not a word we use here. Perhaps you could tell us the last place you went to school."

"Yes, Ma'am," the girl said. "Hamburg, Germany."

"That's very interesting." Miss Harvey opened the book on her desk. This is the way she signals that she is through with you. Dinah wasn't receiving. After a minute, Miss Harvey looked up again. Dinah was still standing beside her seat, very straight, as if she were a soldier waiting to be inspected. "You may sit down, Dinah," Miss Harvey said, with a desperate edge coming into her voice.

"Thank you, Ma'am," Dinah replied. It's almost impossible to make rubber heels click, but Dinah came as close to it as anyone could. Then she slid briskly into her seat. Miss Harvey winced as if something hurt her. She didn't call Dinah down again but flattened the pages of the book with her open palm and began the lesson. She sounded as if she were mad at the multiplication table, but I knew better.

All that morning I watched Dinah Dobbins in a fog of amazement. That girl was hard to believe. Every time a teacher asked a question, her hand was the first one up. If she was called on, she leaped to her feet and stood at attention beside her desk to give her answer. She was almost always right, but there was something about the way she gave her answers that made me think they don't send kids to the office for impudence in Hamburg, Germany.

Take rivers, which is what we were studying in geography. When Mrs. Ferguson asked for a list of major European rivers, Dinah rattled them off by country as if they were the *A, B, C*'s. Mrs. Ferguson smiled her approval and said, "You must like rivers, Dinah."

"I hate them," Dinah replied. "Most of them smell like sewers."

"The Missouri River doesn't." Jim Cane spoke from behind me. "It's a beautiful river."

Dinah turned to stare at him. "You have to be kidding!" she said. "That thing looks like an overgrown, watered-down mud puddle." I turned back to look at Dinah, astonished. I hated to admit it, even to myself, but she was absolutely correct. She could have expressed it a little more tactfully, but she was right about the color of that river and I had never thought about it. I guess when you look at a river all your life and it's the color of chocolate milk, you forget rivers and lakes are supposed to be blue.

Mrs. Ferguson decided to stay out of that. "Class," she said. "You know better than to speak out unless you have raised your hand and been recognized." Her tone was stern and she didn't ask any more questions during the whole period.

Every time I wasn't watching Dinah out of the corner of my eye or trying to cover for the homework I hadn't gotten done, I slid my hand into my jeans pocket and felt that chewed-on twenty dollar bill. The only person I could think of who might have been fooling around the rabbit hutch was that lost boy of Dinah Dobbins. But even if the boy Dinah had been looking for had been down around my rabbit hutch, it was still pretty unlikely he would have that kind of money. I sure didn't see that kind of money when I was a little kid.

Nor do I now, as a matter of fact.

4

Toad, Again!

By careful management I got through until lunch time without coming face to face with Dinah Dobbins. My luck ran out at noon. She saw me walk into the cafeteria and waved at me. I made a kind of wave back and put my things down at the table that was closest to the end of the line without even looking to see who was sitting there.

By the time I got back with my tray and realized that Nat Murphy, his best friend Steve Petersen, and the rest of his gang were at the other end, it was too late to move.

We have three kinds of kids at our school. I'm a town kid because my folks have always lived in

Riverton. My grandparents ran the same grocery store that Dad and Mom run now. The bus kids come in from the farms in the area. A lot of them are really nice and I like them a lot, but you never get to know a bus kid very well because they always leave the minute last period is over. Then, of course, there are the Air Force kids.

Nat's a town boy too, and the tallest person in the sixth grade. He is good at basketball but he isn't anything like as good as he thinks he is. Neither is he anything like as funny as he thinks he is. His idea of humor is to embarrass everybody who gets within the sound of his voice.

My heart fell when I saw Dinah empty her tray and start toward our table. She came and stood right beside me.

"Hi, Toad," she said in an angry, forceful tone. "In case you're interested, I found the boy last night."

"That's good," I said, but I couldn't make myself look up at her. Why did she have to call me that in front of Nat, of all people? I'm blonde like my mom and any little thing turns me bright red. I could feel my face going hot and scarlet, and I just wanted to die. Without even looking, I could imagine Nat's face. When he thinks he has some new way to make somebody miserable, his mouth turns up in an ugly, distorted grin like the mask of comedy that hangs by the left side of the stage in the school auditorium.

"*I* thought it was," she answered in that challenging way of hers. When she turned and walked away, Nat Murphy made a crazy face and whistled shrilly.

Dinah stopped where she was, whirled, and stared at the group sitting around the table as if trying to decide who had done it. Nat and his friends became dead quiet, and the girls looked scared. They stayed that way even after Dinah walked away.

"Toad!" Nat repeated with a roar of laughter as she disappeared into the hall. He was practically shouting. "Toad Potter, that's a kick!" Right away he began to make croaking and belching sounds in his throat so loud that the kids at the other tables all looked around and stared at me.

"Lay off, Nat," Steve said, leaning toward me. "Where in the world did that kid come from, Janie?"

"You heard her in class," I said. "Hamburg, Germany."

"She is one scary female." Steve shook his head. "How did you get mixed up with her?"

"She was on our street last night looking for a little lost boy."

All this time Nat had been making frog noises. That gave him something new to whoop about. "A boy!" he hooted. "What kind of boy would have anything to do with old Orange Shoes?"

I started to say it was her little brother but kept quiet. I felt awful for myself, but I also felt sorry for her in a funny, painful way.

Maybe that's the way kids dress in Germany. Maybe that was even the way they were taught to recite. But whatever made her dress and act like that in class was going to get her more than just whistles at our school.

All this time I was conscious of the twenty dollar bill in my pocket. I couldn't decide what to do about it. Should I just not say anything, or ask Dinah Dobbins if her boy could have stuck in into the wires of my rabbit cage?

I knew I wasn't going to relax until I did *something* about it. I finished drinking my milk and threw away the rest of my lunch.

Dinah was leaning against the wall across from the cafeteria, cradling her books in her arms. A bunch of fifth-grade girls walked by, staring at her. Anyone else would have blushed scarlet. Dinah just looked straight back at them, her face set in an angry frown. I waited until they had passed. When the hall was empty, I went over and pulled out the twenty dollar bill.

"What's that for?" she asked.

"I found it stuck in the wire of my rabbit cage," I told her. "I thought maybe your boy put it there."

Her eyes got very wide for a moment. Then her face darkened with anger. "Now *that*," she said, "is the stupidest thing I ever heard in my life."

She made me sound so ridiculous that I could feel my face turn red. I tried to explain. "I just didn't know of anyone else who had been out there since I fed them yesterday morning."

"And where do you think a four-year-old kid like Blitzen would get money to throw away feeding rabbits?"

"I don't know," I said, catching my breath. "But neither do I know why you always have to be so rude."

"Maybe I am always rude to toads," she snapped right back as she turned away from me.

I had never seen this girl in my life until the night before but something in the way she looked just before she turned away made me hurt inside. I was still staring after her when Steve and Nat and the others came out of the cafeteria. I walked away, pretending I didn't see them.

5

Funny Money

It wasn't raining when I reached home but the sky was dark and boiling with clouds. The house remembered the rain. It felt chilly and damp inside and the air smelled musty. I gave Missy a dog biscuit and fixed myself melted Swiss cheese in some pita bread in the toaster oven. I started my homework right away because I wanted to quit thinking about the way Dinah Dobbins had looked at me.

I had finished my geography and was into my math assignment when the rap came at the back door. Missy beat me there and began to bark ferociously. Through the window, I saw Dinah

Dobbins standing on the steps. She was wearing that poncho again and had added a billed orange cap that matched her shoes. The last thing I wanted to do was open that door, but she was staring back at me through the glass. I sighed, pushed Missy away, and turned the knob.

"Hi," I said, standing inside the screen door.

Missy was carrying on like crazy behind me. Dinah frowned at her, stuck her arm out, waggled a finger toward the dog, and said, "Stay!" in a tone that would have frozen me. It worked on Missy, too. She gulped and swallowed and sat down to quiver without taking her eyes off Dinah.

"Aren't you going to ask me in?"

I stepped back. "I'm sorry. Sure, come on in."

Missy rose and backed off with her tail between her legs. "What's your dog's name?" she asked.

"Missy," I told her.

She knelt, with that poncho making a muddy green puddle around her on the floor. She held out her hand and dropped her voice. "There, Missy, good girl."

"It's short for Miscellaneous," I explained. "Because she's got so many breed lines."

Most people at least grin at that. Dinah ignored me and stayed kneeling there until Missy let her stroke her muzzle and scratch a minute behind her ears. Then she rose and looked at me curiously. "Do you just hang around here all the time by yourself?"

I felt my face getting red again. "There aren't many kids in this end of town. Most of them live on the other side of Main Street."

"But you weren't hanging out with anyone at school today, either."

She sounded like Mom. Mom is forever telling me I spend too much time alone and suggesting that I call somebody and have them over to play. She doesn't understand that you don't just call somebody up unless they've asked you to do it. But what I did with my time wasn't any of Dinah Dobbins' business.

"Is that what you came about?" I asked her.

"Now look who's being rude!" she said. Then she drew her breath deep from her lungs. "I came because I have something I need to ask you."

"Want to come in the living room?"

She shook her head. "I can't stay. I have to get back for the boy." As she spoke she pulled a long box out from under her poncho. She set it on the kitchen table, yanked a rubber band from around it, and took the lid off.

It looked like an ordinary game at first glance. Then I almost went through the floor. Instead of paper play money in those spaces beside the board, this box was crammed full of real bills, tens and twenties and even some fifties.

Dinah was looking at me steadily. I had thought her eyes were plain brown but, when I saw them close like that, they had little gold threads woven in through the colored part. And her eyelashes weren't brown at all but a dead, shiny black.

"Got any ideas where a kid could have gotten hold of these?" she asked.

I was like Missy. I wanted to step back, all the way back, and not admit to myself that I was looking at a ton of real money in that beat-up game box. I shook my head violently.

"No recent bank robberies around here?" she asked. "Any articles in the newspaper about counterfeiters? Any trains been robbed?"

"The train doesn't even stop here any more."

She glared at me. "Don't be such a toad. This is important. Think hard."

"We *have* had a lot of robberies in town," I told her. "But mostly it's just things taken out of houses, not money robberies."

She looked at me thoughtfully. "Have they been

things that would be easy to sell for money?"

I nodded, remembering Dad's using just about the same words when he was talking to Mom: "Whoever is doing this is careful to take only things that are easy to sell."

"Want to compare the bill you showed me at school with one of these?"

I unfolded the twenty I had pulled out of Buckwheat's pen and spread it on the table. She laid another twenty dollar bill from the box beside it and compared them carefully.

"I didn't mean to be rude today," she said, without looking up at me. "I *did* think that the stupidest thing I'd ever heard, but you were right. Except for that place where it's eaten away, your bill looks just as normal as these do."

"Did you ask your brother about the money?"

She glanced at me swiftly. "What makes you think that kid is my brother?"

I stared at her. "Why—*you* said he was."

"Did I?" She studied me a minute and then changed the subject. "What smells so good in here?"

She really was weird. It took me a minute to figure out what she was talking about. "Swiss cheese melted in pocket bread," I told her. "Want some?"

She watched me slice the cheese and stuff the

bread. When the cheese was all runny, I handed the sandwich to her on a napkin. She nodded and ate greedily.

"At school, the food is muck," she said. "At home, Sarge and I have to be the two worst cooks in the world. And if you really must know, Blitzen is a *kind* of a brother—a stepbrother. He was only three and really cute when my mom married his father. That's how I got to be an Air Force brat." Her grin was quick and not very humorous. "Before that I was only the teacher's kid. Mom taught in the American school over in Germany."

She licked some melted cheese off her cheek. "I asked Blitzen where he got the money but I didn't have any luck. He hates me, and since we came over here he's been an absolute monster. If he doesn't want to answer me, he pretends he doesn't hear, or can't understand. Every time I look the other way he runs and hides. He does everything he can think of to make me mad."

"But you used to get along okay?" I asked.

She looked as if she were about to tell me to mind my own business but thought better of it. "We had fun together back in Germany, all four of us. That's ancient history. Now it is the pits, what with Blitzen doing crazy things."

"Maybe he would tell his father," I suggested.

She shook her head. Then this funny thing happened to her face. It looked strange and swollen, as if something was pressing it from inside. "What you don't understand is that my mother's not here yet. I don't dare tell Sarge about this money until I know where it's coming from. It's my job to take care of Blitzen. If he's in trouble, it's my fault."

"I don't think that's fair," I said.

She looked at me, that angry look back again. "There you go," she said, "being a toad again and talking about something you don't even understand. And it's none of your business, anyway."

"Listen—" I began. Who did she think she was to come into my own house and talk like that to me?

She didn't wait to be told off. She just opened the back door and let herself out with the game box hidden under her poncho.

I went to the window and watched her walk off across the yard with her head down. Dinah wasn't the only girl in the world ever to have a stepfather. But the kids I knew called their new fathers "Dad" or "Pop." "Sarge" didn't sound like anything you would call someone you really liked—yet, when she'd spoken of him, her voice had turned gentle.

And Blitzen? What kind of a name was that for a kid?

Then I remembered. That first day she'd told me the boy she was looking for was like lightning. Two of Santa's reindeer in "The Night Before Christmas" had been called Donder and Blitzen, which Mom said meant "thunder and lightning."

I wished I had sent that chewed-up bill home with her. I really didn't want to have anything more to do with it or with her. It didn't make any sense but, as angry and rude as she was, just thinking about her made me want to cry.

6

Blitzen

Mom and Dad were late getting home that Wednesday night. McBride's Jewelry Store had been broken into sometime during the night and the merchants on Main Street had gone down to talk to the chief of police about getting more protection. Mom and Dad discussed it all through dinner. "I feel sorry for Chief Harmon," Dad said. "He has done everything he knows to get to the bottom of this crime wave. He talked to law enforcement people all over the area and instructed his men to watch for any strangers who have no known business in town. Personally, he has always been convinced the thieves were local people who knew the town well. The only houses broken into have been ones where there were real valuables."

"They didn't steal any junker bicycles back in September, either," I reminded him.

Dad nodded at me. "That't right, Janie. But this robbery is a whole new ballgame. This was really grand larceny. The thieves got enough from McBride to buy every kid in town a new bike. And it didn't look like a local job either. The thieves got in through the roof and disabled the alarm system. Very professional. They took all the sterling in stock, a lot of valuable gem stones, and some finished jewelry, including a very expensive diamond bracelet McBride had made on order."

Later, when Mom and I were loading the dishwasher, she asked me how the girl who lived at the Bennett house was getting along at school. "Okay, I guess," I told her, not even wanting to *think* about how Dinah was getting along at school.

"I'm glad to hear that," Mom said. "I've thought about her a lot."

I looked at her, wondering why she should think a lot about a kid she hadn't even met. Because my mom isn't a gossip, I sometimes forget that nothing ever happens in this town that she doesn't hear about. But then, the only way she could avoid knowing all the news would be to wear earplugs. People walk around a grocery store jabbering like crazy to each other, but she almost never tells me anything unless I ask her. And then only if she thinks it's my business.

"The little boy belongs to the father and Dinah belongs to the mother. Her mother was a teacher over in Germany when she met Dinah's new father," I said, really testing to see how much she knew.

"I know," Mom said, wiping off the counter.

"Dinah has to take care of the kid every day after school," I told her. "And he's a handful."

She grinned at me. "I bet some of your baby sitters said the same thing about you before we allowed you to stay by yourself. The family is lucky to have a child old enough to mind the little boy. Sergeants don't make a lot of money," Mom said. "And day school is expensive enough."

"Where does he go during the day?" I asked.

"Babs Nelson's nursery school," Mom said. "The father drops him in the morning and Babs takes him home about four. Babs says he's a nice little boy, very serious and quiet, but nice."

"But where's their mother?" I asked.

"She didn't tell you?" Mom asked, turning to look at me.

I shook my head. "She just said she wasn't here yet."

Mom stood very still a moment as if she were making up her mind. "Janie, you realize all I know is what Babs has told me. Sometimes people talk about things they don't know very much about."

"Yes," I replied.

"I would hate to tell you anything about your little friend's family that wasn't true."

"She's not my little friend," I reminded her. "She's rude and calls me names and is angry all the time."

Mom looked uncomfortable. "I think this is a very hard time for that little girl. Maybe you could be nice to her, whether you like her or not."

"She could do the same thing," I said. "You still haven't told me where her mother is."

"I can only tell you what Babs said," she repeated. "She understood that the mother got very sick on the way here. She had to have an emergency operation and is still recuperating in a hospital back East."

"She will get well and come home?" I asked, wishing I had talked nicer about Dinah.

"I'm sure she will," Mom said. Then she paused and sighed in an exasperated way. "Janie, you know how I hate to talk about other people's business when I have only hearsay to go on. But I really can't imagine that the Air Force would make her husband report back here if she were in any danger."

I guess the word "danger" hit me hard. A minute before I had been going to ask what was the matter with Dinah's mother. I didn't ask because I wasn't sure I wanted to know.

"One of these nights we will have the family over for supper," she said. "It has to be hard for all of them, here in a strange place."

I tried to imagine Dinah at the same dinner table with my mom and dad. Mom sometimes accuses me of being rude. What an eye-opener Dinah would be for her!

Since we live between the Bennett house and school, I watched at the front window hoping I would see Dinah Dobbins go by before I started out. More than anything I didn't want to walk to school with her. I told myself I didn't have to walk to school with anybody who was rude and angry and made such a show of herself that everybody was laughing at her behind her back.

The real reason was that even though I had felt funny and sad ever since I met her, I felt even worse now that I knew why her mother hadn't come to Riverton with her family. What Mom said had sounded reasonable without being too reassuring. There are a lot of scary things in the world but none of them makes you as cold inside as having your mom really sick.

Dinah didn't come and it was getting late so I had to take the chance. The minute I got down to the sidewalk, I saw her walking along the street behind me. I pretended I didn't see her and didn't slow down.

"Toad," she yelled. "Wait up a minute. I want to ask you something."

"My name is Jane," I said, but I stopped and waited.

She caught up and fell into step with me. "Was Blitzen fooling around your rabbit hutches again last night?"

I shook my head. "Not that I know of. Missy would have raised a fuss if anyone was out there. Why do you ask?"

She sighed. "That kid is such a mess. I turned my back one minute last night and he disappeared again. Just as I started out to look for him, he turned up at the back door, all covered over with mud. I barely got him cleaned up before Sarge got home."

"Did he say where he'd been?"

She tightened her lips. "Playing with his rabbits."

"I'm the only one around here with pet rabbits," I told her.

"Blitzen is hateful to me but he isn't usually a liar."

"Maybe he's chasing wild ones," I suggested. "There are millions of those around."

She snorted. "If so, he was chasing them through mud puddles," she said bitterly, "But anyway, I've decided where that money is coming from. It's counterfeit. Somewhere around here, some criminal is printing that stuff up and Blitzen has stumbled onto where he keeps it."

"That can't be right," I said.

She glared at me. "How do you know so much?"

"I don't know so much," I told her. "But I do know that can't be counterfeit money. If it was, all the bills would be the same. You know, all twenties, or all tens, like that."

"How come?" she challenged me.

"Because a counterfeiter has to have a separate plate for every denomination of bill and that would be too expensive."

"How come you know all that?"

"I asked my dad," I told her.

"You what?" she shouted at me.

"I asked my dad," I repeated. "He owns a store. They were talking about the robbery at the jewelry store and I asked him if he had heard about any counterfeit money going around. He said he hadn't and asked what denomination it was supposed to be. When I told him it was all kinds, he told me about the plates."

She stood still with her hands balled into fists at her sides. If she hadn't looked so mad, I'd have thought she was going to cry. "You really *are* a toad, aren't you? And I guess you blabbed about that box of money and the whole thing!"

"Hey," I said. "Lay off me. I didn't say anything about your money. I just asked him about counterfeiters."

"But you know he's suspicious."

"I don't know anything of the sort. And I also don't know why I even try to help you. I should know all you're going to do is yell at me and act as if I didn't have a single brain in my entire head."

She looked at me and then away. "Okay, Toad. I'm sorry."

"Jane," I corrected her.

"Nobody calls you Jane but the teachers," she said.

"Nobody calls me Toad but you," I told her.

"Yes, they do," she replied. "That big kid with the voice like a donkey calls you that. I heard him."

I was about to tell her Nat would never have started except for her when we reached the corner by school. She looked at me and said, "You can go on ahead."

It was tempting. She was offering me a chance to get into school without anybody seeing us together. It was tempting but it was also pretty insulting. "Why should I do that?" I asked her.

She sneered at me. "Who are you kidding? You know you don't want those other kids thinking you've taken up with anybody as rude as you think I am."

"It's not how rude I think you are," I told her. "You *are* rude. You go stamping around mad all the time, just looking for a fight."

"Then why do you want to walk with me?" she asked, halfway smiling.

"I have a perfect right to walk with anyone I want to."

"So do I," she said.

As she spoke, she turned. Her orange sneakers squeaked angrily on the wet sidewalk as she walked away and left me standing there.

School was pretty uneventful until halfway through geography class, which is late in the day. We had turned in homework at the beginning of class. Mrs. Ferguson was grading our work while one of the girls was reading her report out loud. I saw Mrs. Ferguson frown as she opened one of the workbooks, then look up at Dinah. She frowned again and, when the report was through, called Dinah up to her desk.

She tried to keep her voice low but, by the sixth grade, we were skilled eavesdroppers. "Are these yours?" she asked.

Everybody was craning to see what Mrs. Ferguson was talking about.

"No, Ma'am," Dinah said in her stiff way.

"Then what are they doing in your geography workbook?" Mrs. Ferguson asked.

"They must have been put in there by mistake," Dinah said.

"But they aren't yours? Grocery money, perhaps?"

"No, Ma'am," Dinah said, still not looking down at the stack of paper money that was stuffed in between two pages of her workbook.

"What do you think we should do about them?" Mrs. Ferguson asked.

"I have no idea."

"I will have them put into an envelope in the office safe," Mrs. Ferguson said. "They can be kept there until somebody claims them." She paused. "You are *sure* they aren't yours?"

"I am positive, Ma'am," Dinah said, still looking straight ahead.

Mrs. Ferguson counted the bills, sealed them in an envelope, and asked Betsy Zimmer to take them to the office. I didn't look at Dinah as she sat down, but I knew she must be dying of embarrassment over there in her seat.

I knew this town better than she did. If she didn't talk to her dad about that money, someone was going to beat her to it. I *had* to talk her into telling her stepfather what was going on, no matter how upset he got.

I tried to catch her eye to signal her to wait for me when we were dismissed. Instead she sat there looking straight ahead at nothing. The minute the bell rang, she was out the door and gone.

7

Cold Oatmeal

Dinah got clear away before I could catch her. I didn't really have time to fool with her anyway because it was Thursday, which meant I had to go by the store for Miss Foster's order.

"Any word about the jewel robbery?" I asked Mom as she handed me the shopping bag with Miss Foster's things in it.

Mom smiled at me and shook her head. "Not unless you count gossip. Every time someone mentions it in the store, the value of the jewelry has gone up a few thousand dollars." She grinned and stuck a candy bar in my pocket and patted my cheek.

Why did everything in the world make me think of that rude Dinah Dobbins? When I smelled the hand lotion that Mom always uses, I wanted to catch her hand tight. What if she were sick and off somewhere like Dinah's mother? I couldn't stand it, that's what. I really couldn't stand it!

Miss Foster had apparently been watching for me. I saw her face, shadowy behind the glass, from way down the walk. She had the front door open before I stepped up onto the porch.

"There you are, Jane," she said, standing back to let me come in. "I don't know what I'd do without you and your folks."

Her voice is always quavery. That day it was bouncing around all over. Even though she was using her cane, she was unsteady on her feet as she led me into the kitchen. As soon as we got there, she went to the window and looked out into the back yard.

"What's the matter?" I asked. She shook her head and let herself down into a chair by the table.

"I've been watching for Mr. Buck all day to do a little job for me," she said. "Have you talked to him lately?"

I hesitated, then nodded. "Just night before last."

"Did he say anything peculiar?"

Actually, he had *done* something peculiar, but I didn't want to tell her about his grabbing me out there in the dark unless I had to.

"I guess he did," I said. "He asked me if I had been prowling around in the orchard at night. I told him I hadn't, but he still seemed pretty upset."

She nodded. "He talked to me about that, too. He came in here yesterday so angry that he frightened me. I told him it was silly to make a big fuss about a prowler. What could be out there that anyone would want to take?"

"Has Mr. Jeremy seen anybody strange?" I asked.

She shook her head. "I haven't asked him. You know Mr. Jeremy hired Mr. Buck for me, and he gets very upset if I criticize him. I'm not at all satisfied with the way Mr. Buck tends the orchard, but I hate getting into arguments with people."

I nodded. "I don't like that either."

Since she seemed so distracted, I put her milk and butter into the refrigerator just as I would have done at home. When I turned back, she still was sitting by the table, staring at nothing.

"Did you want Mr. Buck for something special?" I asked. "Maybe it's something I can do."

She looked up at me. "My goodness, Janie. It's enough that you keep me in groceries. It's just that the house gets chilly in this wet weather and I am out of wood for the hearth in my parlor. But that's Mr. Buck's job, not yours."

"I can carry wood," I told her.

"So can he," she said a little crossly.

"But you haven't seen him all day?" I asked.

She shook her head. "I can see the light in his quarters from the kitchen window. It was on this morning but I didn't actually see him."

"Let me go out and look for him," I suggested. "If I don't see him, I'll bring a few sticks of wood to hold you over."

"Janie, I hate to bother you like this. I could have gone out myself but I'm too unsteady on my feet on wet ground."

"You know I don't mind," I told her.

She followed me to the back door and flipped on the floodlight. "You'll be careful, won't you?"

I nodded, but wished she hadn't said anything.

It was more dusky than dark out there but the daylight was fading fast. The floodlight wasn't aimed very well. It lit the back steps but nothing beyond. I wished Miss Foster had offered me a flashlight but I didn't want to go back for one. I circled the raspberry bramble and walked along the path toward the stable where Mr. Buck lived. I startled a crow from the pear grove on my left. I jumped a little when he flapped into the air, squawking at me. After that I was really jumpy. I think I even squeaked when a rabbit broke from the tangle of brush and zigzagged across the path, to disappear under the foundation of the tack room at the end of the stable.

I knocked on the tack-room door first and called Mr. Buck's name. When nobody answered, I knocked again and called louder. The crow and a bunch of his friends answered me, but no sound came from inside. The door creaked as I pushed it open. The place was dead dark. I groped for the light switch inside the door and snapped it a couple of times. Nothing happened. If Miss Foster had seen a light earlier, the bulb must have burned out since morning.

Then I really *needed* the flashlight. I stood a long time staring around the room, waiting for my eyes to adjust to the dark. Mr. Buck's clothes were hanging along one wall on a broomstick supported on two clamps. His bed, empty but with the covers turned back, was on the opposite wall.

The floor was covered with an old dusty rug. When I moved, the floor creaked and I imagined rustling sounds.

At the far end of the room, under the window,

Mr. Buck had put together a really simple kitchen out of wooden apple crates. A little portable refrigerator sat in the lower box. A two-burner hot plate sat on the box above it. A teakettle was on the left burner. There was something thick and whitish in it—oatmeal, I realized, oatmeal with raisins, the way I like it. A wooden chair stood by a card table that had a lot of stuff on it—a pile of newspapers, a pair of metal-rimmed glasses, and a pipe with a leather tobacco pouch.

Since there was no place in that room where Mr. Buck could be hiding, I turned back to the door, surprised to realize my heart was beating faster than usual.

In another minute I would have been out the door. But as I paused, I heard the crows begin to scream a warning again. Somebody had to be moving out there to startle them like that. Mr. Buck, I thought, and pushed the door open.

The only light was clear off at the back door of Haverhill House where Miss Foster was probably still standing and waiting for me. Even though I could see nothing in the tangle of the orchard, I had that same spooky feeling as on the night Mr. Buck grabbed me. I stood very still and stared around at the darkness.

I almost didn't believe the kid when I did see him. He was pressed against the trunk of an apple tree, watching me. He stood as motionless as I, staring at me without even blinking. He was little but solid looking, dressed in jeans with a dark matching jacket. He wasn't smiling either, just staring.

"Hi," I said, walking toward him.

He kept on watching me. This had to be Dinah's brother, since no other little kid lived up on that hill. I almost called him Blitzen but hesitated. That might be only a name she called him, the way she called me Toad. If he really hated her, the way she said, using the name might scare him away.

"Have you seen the man who lives here?" I asked.

He tightened his lips together and nodded.

"Where did he go?"

He had been bracing himself against the tree. He pulled one arm out and pointed almost straight at me. I looked around, trying to figure out where he meant. But there was nothing behind me except the empty tack room I had just left.

I heard a rustling and turned back. I couldn't believe my eyes. That kid was gone. Just that quick, he had taken off in the direction of the house. The only reason I knew where he had gone was because the nervous little birds that stay all winter were fluttering wildly in the bushes along the path.

I was still looking after him when I heard Mr. Buck's voice behind me. "There's Jane Potter again," he said, his tone gruff and annoyed. "What are you doing, prowling around out here in the dark?"

I stared at him as he stood by the open door of the tack room as if he had just come out of it.

"You scared me," I said, stepping back. Then I caught myself. "Miss Foster sent me out to ask you to bring in firewood."

"Did she now?" he asked, studying my face as if he thought he could catch me in a lie.

"Yes, she did," I told him. He hadn't moved, but I didn't want him to. "I offered to bring her some if you were busy."

He relaxed at my words. "It's enough that you haul her groceries clear up here. You run along and tell her I'm coming with the wood."

I turned and shot down the path as fast as Blitzen had.

Miss Foster was waiting in the open back door. She had pulled a shawl around her shoulders against the chill.

"Janie!" she cried, when I came into the light. "I am so sorry to have sent you out there in the dark.

I began to worry as soon as you left. Did you see any sign of Mr. Buck?"

I nodded. "I ran into him and he's bringing your wood."

She thanked me again and invited me in to warm up. "You're actually trembling," she said with concern.

There wasn't any point in telling her my trembling had nothing to do with the cold.

8

Helmut

As I came around the porch of Haverhill House to start for home, I saw Dinah marching up the front walk. She was scowling. She kept looking back and forth and peering into the shrubbery, obviously looking for Blitzen.

She glanced up when I spoke. "This time I saw him," I told her.

"Back up there?" she asked.

I nodded. "But he's gone now. I thought he came this way."

She sighed. "He could even have gone on home."

"Why don't you call him?" I asked.

"What a toad you are," she said disgustedly. "I

already told you he hates me. He wouldn't answer me for his life."

I decided to ignore that toad.

"Well, he *is* fast as lightning," I said. "Is Blitzen his real name?"

She glared at me. "Of course not. But his name is even stupider than that. It's Helmut."

"That's not a stupid name," I told her. "It just sounds German."

She nodded. "His mother was German."

"Was?" I asked.

"Not that it's any of your business, but she died," she snapped.

I swallowed hard. I know about mothers and I know about death. I just don't like to think about the two things together. Just hearing that Blitzen's mom had died made me hurt inside. It was extra awful to think about a little kid like that having his mother die. As Dinah started back down the hill beside me, I heard Missy's bark, muffled because she was locked inside the house. I started walking faster.

"What's the hurry?" Dinah asked.

"My dog only barks like that if something or someone is in the yard. I'm always afraid some wild animal from the game preserve has come after my rabbits."

"Boy, you never run out of things to be afraid of, do you?"

I wished I hadn't even told her about seeing her brother. Maybe she would still be up there prowling around the orchard instead of thinking of one rude thing after another to say to me.

"See what a toad you are?" she goaded me. "You don't even argue back. You're afraid of that big conceited Nat Murphy at school. You're even afraid to make friends with anybody."

"If you are talking about yourself, I'm not afraid. Maybe I don't want to have a rude, peculiar person like you for a friend. And like I told you ten million times, my name is Jane."

"Sure, Toad," she said. "Don't you know that just thinking about bad things makes them happen?"

"Bad things *are* going to happen to you that you're not even thinking about," I told her. "Everybody is going to find out that your brother is taking money from somewhere. Mrs. Ferguson has probably told twenty people about finding all that money in your geography workbook."

She stopped and stared at me. "Why would she do that?"

I shrugged. "I don't know anything about Hamburg, Germany, whether it's a little town or a big one, even. But I do know this town and the people in it. People talk about unusual things that happen around here. I bet Mrs. Ferguson wasn't out of that school building before every teacher heard about it. I bet she wasn't even home to her own house before it was all over town. Nobody ever keeps a secret in this town."

"That's what you think!" she said angrily. "But then you always think you know about twice as much as you do. You just *want* her to tell everybody. You just *want* me to get into trouble. Toad!"

That was too many toads. I was really sick of her telling me how I felt and thought about everything. I was sick enough of *her* not to hold back how I really felt.

"You're just crazy if you think that," I told her. "Why would it matter to me what happens to you? You're rude and awful and I hate it when you call me names, but I don't even *care* enough about you to get you in trouble. If I had wanted to do that, I would have shown that twenty dollar bill to my folks. I would have told them about that game box full of real money you brought to the house. In fact, if you want to know the truth, I feel sorry for you. I just want your mother to get well and come home so you won't be so mad and unhappy all the time. You talk about being scared. Nobody's as mad as you are unless they are really scared of something."

She turned and stared at me. "My mother," she whispered. "What do you know about my mother? Who told you anything about my mother?"

When I didn't answer, she got puffy with anger and stepped real close to me. "Answer me, what do you know about my mother?"

I'd never been slapped before. Never in my whole life had I ever been slapped. But Dinah Dobbins stood there in the dark and slapped me in the face as hard as she could hit. I couldn't believe it. I just stared at her and put my hand to my cheek, which felt hard all of a sudden and was stinging. There isn't anything to say to anyone who hits you like that. I turned and ran across the yard fast without looking at her again. Sometimes if you think you are going to cry, you can keep from it by promising yourself things. I whispered the promises out loud in my own mind.

I would never look at Dinah Dobbins again.

I would never speak to Dinah Dobbins again.

If Dinah Dobbins said one more word to me, I would start to scream and drown her out and go home and lock the door against her. But what the promises couldn't do was stop the tears from running down over the stinging skin of my face where she had left the marks of her fingers in bright red stripes.

"Toad," I heard her shouting. "Come back, Toad. I'm sorry."

She was coming behind me and I ran even faster. Missy had been barking so long that her voice was hoarse. As I reached my back door, I could hear her hurling herself against the inside, bruising herself the same way Dinah had bruised me.

"Please, Toad, please," Dinah wailed behind me. I paused, unable to believe my ears. She was crying, too. I shook my head. I couldn't care. I couldn't allow myself to care. I needed to open the door and get inside with Missy. But I couldn't get that silly key out from inside my sweater because Dinah kept grabbing at my hands and begging me to listen.

"I *am* afraid," she whispered in that jerky way you do when you are sobbing. "I'm afraid about Mama. I'm afraid she might die like Blitzen's mother did. His mother had an operation too, but she never got well. It wasn't the same kind of operation, but I can't take any chances. We made a deal, Mama and I. When she got sick and they were taking her off the plane to the hospital, we made a deal."

Missy's barking almost drowned out her words, but I couldn't pretend any longer that I didn't hear

her. "I don't understand this about a deal," I stammered.

She shook her head. "When Mama kissed me good-bye, she said my job was to take care of Blitzen and not worry Sarge. If I did that, she wouldn't have to worry but could just get well and come back home to us so we could all have fun together like we did before. Don't you see, Toad? I *have* to keep my end of our deal or Mama might never come back to us."

As I stared at her, the way she had acted ever since I met her made sense to me for the first time. Maybe it wasn't good sense, but she was only an eleven-year-old kid like me. Whether her mother was sick enough to die wasn't the point. As long as Dinah was afraid of that happening, she would be scared-angry, a feeling I knew. And this business about making a deal with her mother was the kind of thing I had done all my life, except never with anything so important.

As I looked at her, I could see the end of the rabbit hutches against the smokehouse. Blitzen was there, standing absolutely still, watching us. Missy must have heard him and that's why she was barking. The light from the street lamp angled across the back yard, barely touching the end of the hutches.

Blitzen was holding something very round and shiny in one hand. I stared at it, realizing it sparkled too much to be a toy.

I didn't even whisper. It was more that I breathed the words carefully so that Dinah alone could hear them.

"Dinah. Be very quiet. Don't even look around. Just stay here and let me talk to your brother."

She winked hard against the tears and stirred. "Don't move," I told her. "Don't even turn around."

I stood and watched him another minute until I could be sure my voice would sound normal. Then I spoke softly as I went toward him. "Hi, Helmut," I said. "Are you having fun feeding the rabbits?"

He nodded, and the tiniest little upturn came at the corners of his mouth.

"Did they like what you brought them?" I asked.

He shook his head and held out the shiny thing into the light. It was a bracelet, a very shiny white bracelet set with stones that sparkled in the light like diamonds.

"What they *really* like is carrots," I told him. "Do you want to come get some carrots for them? I have some in the house."

He looked at Dinah warily. His expression showed more fear than hate. Then he dropped the bracelet on the ground and walked toward me, staying a long way out of Dinah's reach. She stood very still while I got the door unlocked, shoved Missy back, and went inside with Blitzen following me.

Only then did I turn and whisper to her, "Look at what he dropped out there."

In the light, the kid was darling. He was very round faced, with pale, clear blue eyes and a mop of wavy blond hair. Dinah had called him tubby. He was more sturdy than fat, with a thick chest and solid square hands. He watched me wash the carrots and smiled up at me when I opened the door for him to take them back to the hutch.

Dinah, with the diamond bracelet in her hand, stood silently, staring at me with a sick, defeated expression.

"He's found where the thieves hide their loot," she said in a dull tone of voice. "If they catch him, there's no telling what they would do to him."

I nodded because I was thinking the same thing.

"Maybe we can talk him into taking us where he's been getting these things," I told her. "Somehow he has that place all mixed up with rabbits in his mind."

"He hates me," she said dully. "He'll never tell me."

I almost told her that he didn't hate her as much as he was scared of her, but it wasn't important right then. "Maybe he'll let me know where his rabbits are," I suggested. "I can at least give it a try."

9

Hiding Places

Blitzen came back to where Dinah and I were waiting by the back door. "They liked those carrots," he said contentedly. "I like carrots, too."

Dinah opened her mouth but I shook my head at her. "We gave all the carrots we had to the rabbits," I told him. Then I remembered Dinah's being hungry and having the cheese on pita bread that day. "Do you like cheese?"

His eyes widened and he grinned. "Come on inside," I said, holding Missy's collar with one hand. "We'll all have cheese sandwiches." He looked doubtfully at Dinah as he went past her.

"TV?" I asked him. Another delighted smile.

Blitzen sat in the living room on the couch and watched cartoons while he ate his sandwich. Missy sat right in front of him, bouncing around on her rear and whining.

I motioned Dinah into a kitchen chair and put a sandwich in front of her, too. She sat down and frowned at her plate. "I don't understand what you mean by Blitzen showing you where his rabbits are," she admitted. "You know he doesn't have any. As you pointed out, you're the only one around with rabbits."

"Pet rabbits," I corrected her. "There are rabbits all over Nebraska. They especially like it here in town, where there are fruit trees and garden plants to eat. When I was little I spent hours trying to get close to wild rabbits. I could freeze with the best of them, and I always called them 'my rabbits' when I talked about them to Mom and Dad."

"Okay," she nodded. "Go on."

"Don't you see?" I asked her. "First Blitzen tried to feed the money to the rabbits. Then tonight he was trying to get them to take that bracelet. Remember, you said he came home last night all over mud and told you he had been playing with his rabbits? I think he found the money and that jewelry somewhere that he associates with rabbits.

"The only time I really saw that kid, he was up in back of Haverhill House. And I think he's been there prowling when I haven't seen him."

I told her about the time I'd thought there was someone else on the porch and how Mr. Buck had asked me if I'd been going around up there in the dark.

"Blitzen never has been afraid of the dark. He's not afraid of anything."

"But you," I reminded her.

She flushed a little, then stared at me thoughtfully. "You told me an old woman lives there. Maybe she's a hermit and a miser and Blitzen has found where she hides her treasures."

I shook my head. "Even if Miss Foster were those things, and I know she isn't, she wouldn't hide anything out in the orchard. She has to walk with a cane and barely ever goes off her porch because she's unsteady on her feet."

Blitzen appeared at the kitchen door. "I'm thirsty now," he told me. I filled a glass with milk for him and carried it in to the coffee table in front of the TV.

Dinah was frowning thoughtfully when I got back. "The day we moved in, some man was telling Sarge about the tunnels up under Haverhill House.

He said the river pirates hid stolen things in them until they got a chance to ship them downriver and sell them. Are those tunnels still there?"

"As far as anybody knows, but they were sealed up a long time ago," I told her. "My friend Peter Miller and I spent two whole summers searching for the entrances along the riverbank."

"But you never found them?"

I shook my head. "We didn't but we were sure we were close. Then Peter's father was transferred and he had to move away."

"You mean you never went back on your own to look?"

I felt myself flush. "You can call me a coward if you want, but crawling back in under that hill above the river would be a stupid thing to do by myself." I glared at her. "Okay, I was scared, too."

She ducked her head to try to hide her grin. "That sounds more like good sense," she agreed. "What made you think you were getting close?"

"There are big round drains set along the bank of the river just above the waterline. They were put in to carry off the water that gathers on the hill when it rains or the snow melts. Peter and I decided the opening had to be through the end of one of them."

"That sounds logical enough," Dinah said. "And it doesn't sound all that dangerous."

"Except that nobody takes care of those drains. During flood times, the river has backed up in there, leaving a lot of mud and debris. Even after you clear your way through that, you can go only so far before you come to a mesh, like a screen. Every drain Peter and I explored, and there were three of them, had meshes soldered on so you couldn't get through to the other side. We were sure we were going to find one that wasn't soldered shut, and that one would be the entrance to the tunnel."

"Blitzen isn't scared of anything," she repeated.

"Are you suggesting that Blitzen has been finding the money and jewelry in that old tunnel?" I asked. "That isn't possible. The money he tried to get Buckwheat to eat was a fairly new bill. It was printed only a few years ago."

"You're the one who told me about the crime wave here in Riverton. Maybe the robbers are using the old tunnel as a hiding place until they get a chance to smuggle it out of town."

"Wow!" I said. "What an idea. You know, in the old days they had people come to the opening of the tunnel there on the riverbank. They came in boats at night to carry their loot away. They could even be doing that now!" Then I shook my head. "This is crazy, Dinah. We started talking about rabbits and ended up making wild guesses about the old pirate tunnels. But you could be right about the stuff coming from the robberies here in town. And that would be easy enough to check. Mr. McBride could tell us if that bracelet was part of the merchandise he had stolen."

Dinah's face darkened. "We have to find the place before we talk to anybody. Remember me? I'm the kid who's supposed to be watching over that little monster. Tell me again where you saw Blitzen up around Haverhill House."

"At the edge of the orchard, just across the path from the tack room at the stable. I had been in there looking for Mr. Buck and, when I came out, he was leaning against a tree, watching me."

"Is that a place you would see wild rabbits?" she asked.

I stared at her and then whistled softly. "There was a rabbit. When I went up to look for Mr. Buck, the crows started yelling at me and a rabbit ran across that path and went into a hole in the foundation of the tack room."

"Listen, Toad," she said, leaning toward me. "Blitzen likes you. Do you think you could talk him into showing you his rabbits now? Maybe he would lead you to the place where the money and jewelry are hidden."

I looked up at the kitchen clock. "It's five-thirty," I said.

"So what has that got to do with anything?" she asked, her voice lapsing into that old crossness.

"My folks close the store at six and come straight home, that's what!" I told her. "If I'm not here, they'll be really upset. They know I'm through delivering Miss Foster's things by four o'clock."

"Half an hour is a long time," she coaxed.

"There's always tomorrow," I reminded her.

"For you maybe," she said. "If you are right about Mrs. Ferguson's blabbing all over town about that money, I could be in Dutch the minute Sarge gets home from the base."

"We could leave a note," I decided out loud.

"Not we." She shook her head. "Blitzen won't take you there if I'm along. He hates me," she said again.

"Why?" I asked. Her face turned very red and looked swollen, the way it had before. I realized she was fighting tears because that's the way my face feels when I am trying hard not to cry. "Have you hit that kid the way you hit me?" I asked, angry all over again.

She nodded and wouldn't look at me. "I didn't mean to. It's just that he scared me so bad when he started running away."

I stood up and reached for my parka. "Now who's a toad?" I asked her. "I'll see what I can get out of Blitzen. You stay here with Missy, and if my folks come before we get back, tell them I'm taking care of your little brother for you. It won't exactly be a lie."

10

The Tack Room

Dinah and Blitzen together were even more confusing to me than they had been apart.

Every time I thought about Dinah's rudeness and her anger and how she had hit this little kid, I just boiled. It wasn't Blitzen's fault that Dinah's mother was sick. And it wasn't fair for her to take out her anger and fear on him. How could he know that every time he ran away or got into mischief, Dinah got scared all over again because she felt her mother's life depended on her keeping her part of their whispered bargain?

In fairness to Dinah, the kid was a handful. But he had already lost his own mother. Maybe he was as scared of losing Dinah's mother as Dinah herself was. Maybe he was running away from his own fear as much as he was trying to escape Dinah's anger.

It hurt just to try to sort it out. I couldn't even imagine how panicked and angry I would be if I thought I might lose Mom. And if I honestly thought her life depended on my doing a hard thing well, as Dinah felt her mother's did, how would I act? I wasn't sure I could handle my fear any better than Dinah was doing.

And I really liked Blitzen. I liked the solid, reasonable way he stood and thought when I talked to him about taking me to see his rabbits. In fact, his eyes sparkled when he realized that I cared about something of his.

I first saw the fog when we started out to get the flashlight Dad keeps on the shelf by the rabbit hutches.

Fog is the only thing I know of that flows up instead of down. While we were talking, the fog had risen from the face of the river. I have seen it come like that before. It moves almost like a living thing, gradually filling up Main Street before it starts to weave up the hill and around the houses that flank the downtown section. The light in front of our store turns fuzzy in it, becoming a fused mass instead of the letters that spell POTTER'S FINE GROCERIES. New wisps of fog were trailing up the path that led to Haverhill House. Maybe that was all right. If Mr. Buck was out there watching for prowlers, he wasn't nearly as apt to see Blitzen and me and yell at us.

Blitzen slid his hand into mine. "What's that smoky white stuff?" he asked.

"Fog," I told him. "The air turns like that when it is carrying a lot of water. Our fogs come up from the river, but they are still just air." He looked uncertainly at me. When I smiled, he tightened his grip on my hand.

"Toad," he said, in a tone that was almost loving. I groaned silently and squeezed his hand back. I loved the trusting way he said my name, even if it wasn't my name at all.

When I reached for the flashlight, Buckwheat jumped to the front of the cage to greet me. I pressed my hand against the wire to rub the side of his face.

"My rabbits won't let me touch them," Blitzen said. "They won't even let me get close. They just run and hide." His tone was wistful.

"Maybe someday," I told him.

By the time we got halfway up the walk to Haverhill House, the porch was buried in mist. It reached almost to the light in the high window of the room where Mr. Jeremy does the writing for his history book. If there was a light on in the parlor, I couldn't see it from the front of the house.

I was glad Blitzen was clinging to my hand. That way I could lead him where I knew it would be safe, around the corner of the porch, past the raspberry brambles, and in back of the root cellar.

The light was on in Miss Foster's kitchen. It shone square into the fog-filled back yard, and I figured she was making dinner for herself and Mr. Jeremy. I was sure he took his meals with her, because she started buying lots more groceries than usual as soon as he came to stay there to do his research. When Mr. Jeremy first arrived, I heard Dad tell Mom that probably Miss Foster had let a perfect stranger into her house because she needed the extra income.

Those nervous, twittery little birds fluttered and chirped as Blitzen and I got to the edge of the orchard. When Blitzen reached the tree across from the tack room where I had seen him that first time, he paused and stood very still. Then he nodded and put his finger to his lips. The light was on in the

tack room. Mr. Buck must have put in a new bulb.

After a minute Blitzen tugged his hand away and motioned for me to follow him. He crouched below the level of the window to run swiftly toward the back of the tack room. I followed, suddenly breathless. Maybe he could just show me where the rabbit was. Maybe he could point out the hole, and then we could come back and really search when it was daylight.

Before I even opened my mouth to suggest it, Blitzen disappeared behind the tack room. By the time I turned the corner, he was squatting by the back wall of the building. I knelt beside him and looked at a narrow hole between the foundation stones. "In there," he whispered.

In a way I was relieved. It wasn't possible for either of us to squeeze through a hole that small. But even as I drew that breath of relief, Blitzen tugged at one of the stones and rolled it away. Then he lay down on the ground and wriggled through the opening, feet first and flat on his back. I sat on my heels wishing I had never started this whole thing. Then his face appeared at the hole, looking out at me.

I knew I wouldn't fit. I *hoped* I wouldn't fit. But I had to try, after selling Blitzen that bill of goods about wanting to see where his rabbits lived. I lay on my back and got my legs and hips between the stones and into the crawl space under the floor without any trouble. I had to fold my shoulders in to get them through, but in a moment I made it. I was sure I had scrape marks on the sleeves of my jacket.

The floor of the tack room above us wasn't well made. Along one wall a streak of light shone into the cluttered darkness around us. Blitzen was already worming his way off, flat on his belly. I started after him, hating every minute of it.

It smelled awful down there, like dead mice with the mustiness of mildew mixed in. Even when I kept my face down, I could feel sticky things grab at my hair. I just knew they were spider webs. I hate spiders worse than almost anything because they have so many more legs than any creature needs and they move so fast, sometimes even jumping. I was also absolutely sure these were the webs of the black widow spiders that like dark wet places and are poisonous to old people and children.

Ahead of me, Blitzen startled a rodent that squeaked and fled away, rustling as it ran. I wished I could catch up with Blitzen but he was moving much faster than I, as if he knew exactly where he was going. I didn't dare make a sound with that light on above us in Mr. Buck's tack room. In that quiet, I imagined Mr. Buck with his ear pressed to the floor, listening as hard as I was.

When the streaks of lights disappeared from above, I knew we had left the tack room behind. The earth under my hands was different here, damper and not so well packed, and I felt as if we were going downhill. The farther Blitzen crawled, the more scared I got. There was only bare ground above us now. Everything Peter Miller had said about those tunnels being dangerous came back to me.

"Even if they put supports in them all that long time ago," he'd said, "they probably just used wood. Wood can rot and let the ceiling fall right in on you."

And Blitzen kept on crawling.

I was wet all over with a different kind of sweat, a cold sweat that made me shiver. I didn't know whether it was because I was afraid or because there wasn't any air left, but I started having trouble breathing. The only way I could breathe was to pant with my mouth open, the way Missy does when she's hot. Just when I thought I couldn't make myself go a single inch more, Blitzen stopped and I crawled right into his feet.

Before I could figure out why he had stopped, he

moved away and I heard a faint, dull thud. I groped for his feet again but couldn't find him. As I pawed in the darkness, I heard him hiss at me softly from somewhere below. By feeling ahead, I realized I was at the end of the tunnel and he had dropped down to another level. I pressed my hands on the earth where it stopped. There was nothing out there but air. Then his hand came up and he was grabbing at mine. I told myself desperately that the drop couldn't be too far, or he couldn't have made it. I sat on the edge of the shelf a moment, took a deep breath, and let myself down.

Suddenly I could stand up. When I reached as high as I could, I touched the ceiling. We had been in a passageway all that time and now we were in a *real* tunnel and Blitzen was tugging at me to follow.

Peter and I had pictured a tunnel like this. I could reach the top and touch the sides, which meant it was about the size of one of those big drains along the river cliff that we had tried so hard to get into. Blitzen gripped my hand and pulled me after him. Something untidy littered the floor and rustled as we tiptoed along. It was dead black dark but, because Blitzen was so carefully silent, I was afraid to use my flashlight. The silence scared me almost as much as the wet darkness.

I promised myself that if I got out of that place alive I would never even go down into the basement again. And I would never argue with Dinah about being a coward. I *was* a coward, and I didn't even care who knew it. What's more, if Blitzen hadn't been scared the first time he came in there, he was either the bravest little boy in the whole world or the stupidest. Maybe he was both.

As his moist hand kept tugging me forward, it got easier to breath. The air still smelled musty, but a new yet familiar sharpness had been added. Suddenly I recognized that heavy, wet scent. That's the way it smells along the river where it passes the bird sanctuary. That peculiar aroma comes from a spicy weed that grows there by the beach. The thought that we might be getting near the river end of the tunnel scared me all over again. If we ended on the riverbank, we'd have to come back this same way because there aren't many places a human being can climb those dirt embankments. The thought chilled me.

"Blitzen," I whispered, as softly as I could.

He slapped at me as if to warn me and went around a curve in the wall. As I followed him, I gasped to see a dim flow of light up ahead. We were almost out of the tunnel and we *were* very near the river. I could hear the hollow slap of the water against the shoreline.

Blitzen stopped. After a minute, he grabbed my hand and shoved something into it. Paper. He was handing me paper bills! As dim as the light was, I saw him grinning as he pulled handfuls of money out of one of a row of cartons at the side of the tunnel and pushed them at me.

The light appeared without warning. I think I screamed. This was no dim fused light but a glare so intense that, without thinking, I covered my eyes with my hands, letting the paper money flutter to the floor. Even then, circles of color danced inside my closed lids. I heard Blitzen gasp and felt him grab at my jacket.

I recognized Mr. Buck's voice instantly. "What did I tell you?" he snarled. "Now do you believe me?" He was shouting at someone I couldn't see. His words rose angrily, vibrating against the walls of the tunnel. "You were so sure it had to be me! You wouldn't believe it when I told you there was prowlers around. No! *Buck took the money. Buck was into the jewelry.* Look at these kids with their fists full of bills and ask yourself just who has been robbing us blind. They'll have those diamonds on them somewhere too, just see if they don't."

That flood of light was blinding me. Until some-one lunged toward us and caught Blitzen by the arm, I had no idea who Mr. Buck was shouting at. Mr. Jeremy! I stared in disbelief. How had Mr. Jeremy gotten mixed up in this—a writer, a distin-guished historian?

Blitzen was an eel in Mr. Jeremy's arms. I watched him struggle wildly against the man's strength. I'd been right about that little boy. He wasn't tubby. He was just strong and solid and full of fight.

But Mr. Jeremy was a lot bigger, and ruthless besides. He didn't seem to care how much he hurt the kid. I saw him wrench Blitzen's arm up and behind his back and could have cried. Blitzen didn't exactly cry. Instead, he let out an angry howl, bent over at the waist, and buried his teeth in Mr. Jeremy's leg.

Screaming, Mr. Jeremy clutched at his thigh and dropped Blitzen onto the floor of the tunnel with a thud. He was instantly sorry and started yelling. "Catch him, Buck," he shouted. "After him. Grab that little devil before he gets away."

Any other time in my life I would have split laughing. Mr. Buck lumbered after Blitzen like the big bad animal in a Saturday morning cartoon. Blitzen had a good two-yard start on him. The kid ran a few more feet, paused, shoved a carton into Mr. Buck's path, and shot off down the tunnel toward the river, running like a rabbit—like one of his wild rabbits, not my overfed, sleepy pet rabbits. Mr. Buck tripped over the carton, spilling jewelry and loose silver onto the dirt floor. He caught his balance, cursed, and started after Blitzen again.

When Mr. Buck started chasing Blitzen, the glare of the flashlight was off my face for the first time. I caught my breath, turned, and ran back up the tunnel toward the darkness under the hill.

But I'm not any Blitzen. Mr. Jeremy caught me in a few swift steps. He grabbed me by both shoulders and slammed me hard against the side of the tunnel. I cried out with the pain and clung to his arms. It didn't work. I felt my knees buckling and wailed for help. My head really hurt and I remember thinking that he was going to knock me out if he wasn't careful. Then there was nothing.

11

Missy

I heard men talking. Their voices sounded hollow—or a long way away. I held really still because it hurt to move. I'd had headaches before, but nothing like this one. My skull felt as if something were caught in there alive and was trying to beat its way out with a stick. My shoulders ached from where Mr. Jeremy had held them when he banged me against the wall.

Both voices were angry. Mr. Jeremy was cursing at Mr. Buck for not catching "that stupid kid," and Mr. Buck was snarling back at him for letting "the little devil" go in the first place. Being angry didn't keep them from working. I heard the scrape of their feet going back and forth in the tunnel and the sound of things being pushed around.

"Get all those boxes out in front and we'll shut this place up again," Mr. Jeremy ordered.

"We don't have time to move all those rocks back into the drain," Mr. Buck argued. "That kid could bring somebody after us in a matter of minutes."

"He's not much more than a baby," Mr. Jeremy scoffed. "But the girl is different. I don't intend for anybody to find her alive. It would take her about a minute to tell Chief Harmon everything she saw down here. And she's old enough to testify and make a jury believe her. Now get moving. We can be out and away in a shake if you'll quit blabbing and pack this stuff up."

"Keeping the money and jewelry down here was stupid in the first place," Mr. Buck grumbled. "We should have fenced the stuff and used a bank box like we usually do."

"Quit griping and get that tarpaulin off the boat," Mr. Jeremy told him. "It was smart enough until the kids found our stuff. That was a fluke. We wouldn't have found this tunnel ourselves except for old lady Foster giving me the stuff out of her attic. Quit jabbering and start shoving."

"Get a look at the fog," Mr. Buck called, his voice

suddenly fading. "I can't see two feet in this muck."

"That fog's going to help," Mr. Jeremy replied. "Once we get the boat into the current, no one could see up pass even if he was watching the river."

"I hear something," Buck said, his voice low and tense. "It sounds like voices, maybe a motor, too."

For a moment there was silence.

When Mr. Jeremy spoke again, his voice was higher and his words were clipped. "Pitch in with these rocks," he said. "It's probably nothing. Noises sound strange in a pea soup like this. But there's no point in taking chances."

I heard the scape of stones being moved back into the entrance of the drain and began to cry silently. They were going to pen me in here. I would die.

"Do you suppose they'll even find her body?" Mr. Buck asked.

"Who cares, once we're gone?" Mr. Jeremy asked. "She might even get lucky and never wake up. I slammed her head pretty hard against the wall."

I had started to crawl toward the sound of their voices. I stopped. Maybe if they heard me they'd come back and kill me, to keep me quiet. At least I had a fighting chance if I tried to work my way back to the tack room.

Their voices got dimmer. I had to strain to hear.

"There you go." That was Mr. Buck's voice. "The tarp is on tight. Unhook the boat."

"Shove," Mr. Jeremy said after a minute. "Dig that oar in and shove. Those *are* voices and they're getting closer."

"Hey! The water's kicking up and I *do* hear a motor," Mr. Buck whispered tensely.

"Shove," Mr. Jeremy ordered. "It's probably only a fishing launch but let's get out into the fog cover."

When I heard nothing for a while, I crawled toward the stones Mr. Jeremy and Mr. Buck had shoved into the opening of the tunnel. There was absolutely no light. I felt around on the rocks, scratching my hands something awful but not finding any place I could get a grip. The river lapped outside and I heard the pulse like a motor draw very near and then pass by. That must be the fishing launch the men had heard. I could have signaled through the cracks of the rocks if only I'd had a light.

A light!

All that time I hadn't even thought of the flashlight I brought from home. I had still been holding it when Mr. Jeremy grabbed me and shoved me up against the wall. I crawled back along the tunnel, feeling the dirt floor carefully as I went. I was almost excited. If I found the flashlight I could certainly make my way back to the crawl space under the tack room.

My hand touched something sharp that hurt the tips of my fingers. Without even remembering how filthy my hands must be, I popped my fingers into my mouth. Blood. I had cut my fingers on something there on the tunnel floor, something like glass.

"Oh, no," I whimpered, and felt carefully around my knees. The flashlight was there all right, but the glass was broken and, where the little bulb should have been, was something hairy and sharp that cut my finger again, making it start to bleed in a new place.

I was the kid who didn't like to hurt, yet here I was in a blocked-up, spidery tunnel, hurting all over and like to die because I'd gotten mixed up with an Air Force brat, even though I knew better. For once I was too scared even to be angry.

I knew crying was silly, but I couldn't help it. I could die back in this walled-off tunnel and never see my mother again, or Dad, or Missy and the rabbits. I just leaned against that wall and bawled. My shoulders really ached. The more I cried the worse my head hurt, and then my nose began to run. I wanted to howl the way Blitzen had when Mr. Jeremy twisted his arm back.

I didn't even have anything to wipe my nose on,

and Mr. Jeremy and Mr. Buck were right. Blitzen wasn't a whole lot more than a baby. Who would believe him if he told them a crazy story like this? And who would he tell it to, anyway? I'd seen the careful way he avoided Dinah. Fat chance he would tell her anything!

The river began to lap louder against the shore beyond the stones and I heard the pulse of a motor launch again. I stared at the rocks. A tiny thread of light had glimmered there through the cracks for a moment, then gone away.

"Fishing launch," Mr. Jeremy had said. But no fisherman would be flashing his lights on the banks of the river like that. I raced to the stones and tried to pull at them again. If Blitzen had told somebody who believed him, the police would search along the riverbank by boat. That *could* be the searchlight of a police boat looking for the end of the tunnel.

"Help," I screamed. "I'm here. Help! Help!"

Even with the sound of the motorboat fading, I kept on yelling. Without a light, all I had was my voice. And noise travels funny ways in fog. Maybe somebody on the cliff above might even hear me.

The next sound I heard was curious and scary. Rocks and earth rattled and tumbled against the stones barring the entrance to the tunnel. It sounded as if someone, or something, was plunging down that steep cliff, starting avalanches as it came. Whatever it was, it hit the water with such a huge splash that waves sloshed nervously against the shore. The motorboat was far upstream, now only a low pulsing beat I could hardly hear. But, on the other side of the rocks, a dog began scratching and whining and barking in a pitiful, begging way. Missy!

"Missy," I shouted. "Missy, help!"

Her barking changed and the scratching became more intense. She sounded frantic, the way she does when she is trying to dig a prairie dog out of its hole.

I kept calling and Missy kept scratching for what seemed like forever. Then, suddenly, the sound of the boat's motor got louder again, and other voices were shouting. Something scraped hard on the beach, and Dinah Dobbins was yelling, "Toad. Where are you, Toad?"

It took the men about half as long to pull those rocks away as it had taken Mr. Jeremy and Mr. Buck to roll them into the drainpipe. The minute the first rock was free, a flood of brilliance from the boat's searchlight blazed into the tunnel. Before they even made space for one man to come in, Missy scrambled through the rocks, tumbled onto the floor, and was all over me, licking my face and whining, trembling as hard as I was. Finally I got an arm lock around her neck and managed to get to my feet. Then Dad was there, tall and solid and dark against the light. He leaned over and grabbed me in such a hard hug that I almost yelled out because it hurt my shoulders so much. "Janie," he whispered. "Janie."

I looked beyond him to the opening of the tunnel. The light from the boat shone around the whole group of figures. Chief Harmon was there, barking into that radio he carries around with him. Mom was there all alone, bunched over and crying, beside a tall man in uniform who stood with Dinah under one arm and Blitzen under the other.

I started to cry all over again and hugged Dad even though it hurt.

12

Dynamite

Chief Harmon was obviously in a hurry to get rid of us. That police launch wasn't designed to carry such a crowd, but he managed to squeeze us all in, even Missy, who sat dripping under his feet. The chief gunned the motor all the way to the Riverton dock faster than I have ever moved on the river.

"Get that kid dried out," he told Mom, as if she didn't know anything about mothering. "Where can we reach you later?"

"Haverhill House," Dad said quickly. "Miss Foster will have to see Jane for herself to be sure everything's all right."

Chief Harmon looked at me and shook his head. "I'll be around later. I'm hoping you can help with the unanswered questions we have about this case, Jane." He paused. "In the meantime, I can't believe anybody could get *that* many spider webs into one head of blonde hair."

I wanted to shriek at the very idea. Mom just hugged me and laughed.

Every light in Haverhill House seemed to be lit. I recognized Miss Foster's shadow behind the glass in the front door the moment we reached the porch steps. She was outside before we got to the top. "Janie," she cried, and reached for me without even holding on to her cane.

We all crowded there at the door with Missy at my heels. When Miss Foster got a good look at me in the light, she squealed. "Janie! Oh, my goodness."

I knew it was the spider webs and the streaks of dirt on my face that I had smudged with crying.

"We hope you have lots of hot water," Mom said. "Under all that dirt, we think she's okay."

Miss Foster clung to my hand and looked past me to the man who was Dinah and Blitzen's father. "I'm afraid I don't know this gentleman." Her voice was hesitant.

He stepped forward and took her hand. "Sergeant Dobbins," he said. "And these are my children, Dinah and Helmut." He was very tall and thin, and as blond as Helmut. His eyes were blue, too, but stained looking underneath, as if he hadn't slept very well for a long time. Dinah looked dark and strange beside those two blond people. She hadn't said a word to me since we all got into the boat, and she wasn't looking at me now. Instead she just stared down at the floor with her mouth in a funny straight line.

"Come in, come in," Miss Foster said, and her eyes strayed to me again. "There's a bathroom at the top of the stairs, Janie, if you'd like to wash up."

Mom motioned for me to go up but I shook my head. "I want to know what happened."

"There'll be time for that. I'm sure everyone needs a hot drink. Maybe you're even hungry?"

When Miss Foster looked flustered, Mom laughed. "Don't worry about having enough food, Miss Foster. There have to be some advantages to being in the grocery business. Now up those stairs, Janie."

Missy followed me and waited outside the bathroom door, whining every once in a while. Even though that was the fastest bath I've ever taken in my life, Dad had already been to the store and back when I came out, freshly bathed with my hair still damp from toweling.

The hall air was heavy with the smoky sweet smell of bacon and the sharp fragrance of coffee. Everyone was in the kitchen and talking at once. When I got to the door, Blitzen slid off a high stool and ran over to catch me around the waist. I touched his head with my hand.

"How's your arm?" I asked.

He wriggled it at the shoulder and made a face. Then he took my hand. "You okay, Toad?" he asked.

Dad frowned and looked over at me. "What did he call you, Janie?"

"Toad," I said. "It's my new nickname." Dinah flushed a deep red.

"Toad!" Mom repeated, as if she couldn't believe her ears.

"I like it," I told her. "I really truly do."

Fortunately I can eat and listen at the same time. With everybody talking at once, it wasn't easy to figure out what exactly had happened. The one thing that came through right away was that Blitzen and Missy had been the real heroes only because Miss Foster had been "on her toes," as Dad put it.

"When Blitzen came back alone, I knew something awful had happened," Dinah said. "I let Missy out and told her to look for Toad."

"How did Blitzen ever get back to my house?" I asked. "He couldn't have climbed up that cliff from where we were."

"I ran along the bank and then zigzagged," Blitzen replied. "I did that before one time."

Dinah groaned and put her head in her hand.

"I heard the dog barking and saw two children passing the house in that awful fog," Miss Foster said. "With the floodlight on, I caught the barest glimpse of them before they disappeared into the darkness. I was frightened for them because it was so dark. You know it isn't very far from the stables to the edge of the cliff above the river. The only thing I could think to do was phone Mr. and Mrs. Potter at the store."

Dad looked over at me. "Miss Foster had mistaken Dinah for you, Janie," he explained. "We were on the way home and she missed us. She did the next smart thing, which was call Chief Harmon. He was already up in our neighborhood because Sergeant Dobbins had checked with him when he found his own children missing. When Harmon told us about the call from Haverhill House, we picked up the sergeant and all came up together. Dinah and Blitzen were out there starting to crawl under that tack room when we caught them."

"But the boat?" I asked. "How did you know to come with the boat?"

"Blitzen," Dinah said. "He kept saying it would take too long to go through the tunnel to get you and we'd have to go down to the river." She glanced at my dad. "Nobody would have believed him except that he was covered with clay and mud when he got back to your house."

"Missy wouldn't come," Blitzen said. "We tried to pull her but she kept digging under the tack room and we had to go without her."

"It's a good thing we did," Dad said. "Chief Harmon got the launch and we started searching along the river, going up and down. All the rocks looked the same to us, until that last trip downriver. Somehow Missy had made it over the cliff and was trying to tear the world apart to get into that tunnel."

"How in the world did Missy know where you were?" Mom asked me.

I laughed. "I had my mouth pressed to the spaces between two rocks bellowing like a bull," I told her.

"And, as Miss Foster said, it isn't very far from the back of that tack room to the edge of the cliff. My wails must have carried up there."

By the time Chief Harmon's cruiser drove up the hill, we had explained about Blitzen's trying to feed the money to the rabbits and then bringing that diamond bracelet. The chief didn't come in right away but went out toward the stables with another officer who had pulled in behind him in a separate car.

He finally came into the house alone, looking pretty pleased with himself. He accepted coffee gratefully and grinned at us. "Well, we got them. They couldn't go very far in the fog with that little boat loaded like it was. We also found out how they got down into that tunnel. Somebody put a trap door in the floor of that old tack room and covered it with a rug."

Dinah's father looked at me. "I can't believe they meant to leave you there."

"They're mean," Blitzen said. "Jermy and Buck are mean."

"I simply don't understand," Miss Foster said. "Do you mean that Mr. Jeremy wasn't doing research at all?"

Chief Harmon made a noise a little like a snort

and held his mug out to Dad for more coffee. "He was doing research all right. With the excuse of that book, he got into the finest old homes in town to case them for robberies. And most of that stuff is probably gone forever."

"They fenced it," I told them. "This isn't the only town they've done this to."

Dad stared at me. "Fenced?"

"I don't really know what that means," I admitted. "It's just some of the stuff they said when they thought I was knocked out."

"Sounds reasonable." Chief Harmon nodded. "Their boat was loaded with packets of money along with McBride's jewelry and silver. I left it all at the station to be inventoried." He paused and shook his head. "You know, when the robberies first started, my men and I looked at those two very carefully. But no matter who we asked, we got a clean bill of health for Jeremy. In fact, he was everybody's fair-haired boy because he was going to put this town on the map with his history book. Incidentally, McBride may get all of his stuff back, from the way it looks."

"But not my bike," I said crossly.

"Maybe he'd trade you a bicycle for this," Dinah said, fishing in those big putty-colored pants of hers.

Chief Harmon gasped when she laid the diamond bracelet on the table under the light.

"Dinah," her father breathed. "Where in the world did you get that?"

She grinned for the first time. "That's what started this whole thing tonight, Sarge. Blitzen tried to feed this to Toad's rabbits. Instead, Toad talked him into showing her where his rabbits lived."

"But Blitzen doesn't have any rabbits," her father said, looking confused.

"No *pet* rabbits," I corrected him. "When I was little, I used to try to make up with wild rabbits too. I figured he was finding the money and jewelry wherever it was that his rabbits went."

"Kid logic," Chief Harmon said with a chuckle.

"Clever detection," Dinah told him.

Miss Foster was worried about not having dessert until I reminded her of the big carrot cake I had brought in the Tuesday delivery. She had forgotten it but quickly sliced it and offered it around until it was all gone.

You could tell everyone was winding down when the room got quieter. Mom spoke into the silence. "How is your wife getting along, Sergeant Dobbins?"

His smile was broad and sweet and sudden, like

Blitzen's. "She's gaining strength, but it's been a long hard battle. It was a ruptured appendix, you know, and the peritonitis was the scary part. The kids and I wanted to stay with her but she has a real talent at getting her way."

Like Dinah, I thought, without saying it.

"She thought we would all be better off being settled into our new home," he went on. Then he shook his head, laid a hand on Dinah's shoulder, and smiled down at her. "I knew it was tough for all of us, worrying about her and missing her, but I had no idea *how* tough it was on my Dynamite."

I'd never heard that nickname before, but it really fit. Even when Blitzen was leaning sleepily against his father's side, I couldn't imagine calling him anything as tame as Helmut. But Dinah hadn't done badly in nicknaming me, either. I really was a toad when I first met her. Maybe I didn't have warts or catch flies with my tongue, but I had sure been spending my life squatting in a hole looking out at life.

Dinah's face was swelling the way it had when she cried before, but these weren't unhappy tears. She wasn't going to cry any *really* happy tears until her mother came home. But at least she could quit worrying about keeping up her end of the deal. If

I ever saw a father proud of a daughter, it was her Sarge.

"But I had help," Dinah reminded him, looking over at me. "I had Jane."

"Toad," I corrected her.

"Toad," Blitzen echoed softly. His eyes were all the way closed as he leaned back and smudged his father's shirt with the carrot cake from his upper lip.

Books by Mary Francis Shura

Don't Call Me Toad!

The Josie Gambit

The Search for Grissi

Happles and Cinnamunger

The Barkley Street Six-pack

Mister Wolf and Me

The Gray Ghosts of Taylor Ridge

The Riddle of Raven's Gulch

AND THE COMPANION BOOKS

Chester

Eleanor

Jefferson

MARY FRANCIS SHURA has written over twenty books for young people. Born in Kansas, not far from Dodge City, the author has lived in many parts of the United States, including California and Massachusetts. Both of her parents came from early settler families of Missouri.

Aside from writing fiction for young readers and adults, Mary Francis Shura enjoys tennis, chess, reading, and cooking—especially making bread.

The mother of four grown children, the author currently makes her home in the western suburbs of Chicago, in the village of Willowbrook.

Her most recent book is *The Josie Gambit*. Two other titles, *Chester* and *Eleanor*, were selected for Children's Choices by the International Reading Association/Children's Book Council Joint Committee. *The Search for Grissi* won the 1985 Carl Sandburg Literary Arts Award for Children's Literature.

JACQUELINE ROGERS lives in West Redding, Connecticut. She was graduated from the Rhode Island School of Design and teaches at Paier College in Connecticut. She greatly enjoys illustrating children's books.